METAPHORICALLY METAPHORISE

METANAFIC - A NEW GENRE

VEENA J

Made with ♥ on the Notion Press Platform
www.notionpress.com

Dedicated to all new interpretators

Contents

Preface *vii*

Acknowledgements *xi*

Demo *xiii*

1. The Woe Of A Social Butterfly 1

2. Bicyclic Nature 2

3. Illuminating Your Love 3

4. Untold Love Tale 4

5. Ones Bastion 5

6. The Fabric And Fabricator 6

7. Not The Regular Cloud Nine 7

8. Counting Steorra 8

9. Tele – Vision 9

10. Tailess Lizard 10

11. Tot's Mind; Thoughts In Mind 11

12. Valuable Stuffs 12

13. Seasonal Phase 13

14. Stage Of Life 14

15. Just The Two 15

16. When Second Speaks 16

17. The Wealth I Posses 17

18. Budding Actor 18

19. Gushing But Worth It 19

20. Unnoticed Gems 20

21. From My Abyss 21

22. Aren't You Exhausted? 22

23. An Artisan's Silence 23

Contents

24. The Serendipity It Holds 24

25. Gentle Gaintess 25

26. Replaced Versions 27

Author's Bio 53

Preface

As literature students, we are taught to view literature as something beyond than what normal readers do. We are encouraged to take a deeper look at the material than what is there in the writing. We are taught about the structure and the forms of certain writings as well. Like how poets use a lot of metaphors, whereas novelists prefer to present their work in a more descriptive manner. When we get into writing ourselves, we think about what we want to write, think about the form and structure that is usually used for that work, and we tend to stick with the rules. It is rare for us to think about doing something outside the box, something that doesn't completely align with what people are used to reading for the past 3-4 centuries. But it is not impossible. Once in a while, there are people who think to defy the norms set for us. To see if it might work. This book is something that was written to defy those norms.

But defying norms doesn't mean completely ignoring everything, I also did not want to lose any of the traditional devices used to write. I felt like an assorted blend of a lot of those devices would help in bringing this idea to life. Using metaphors, narratives and fiction was the conclusion for this blend. By doing so, in a way, this book would be in a completely new genre. Coming up with a name for that was quite a challenge but after a long thought, the result was something I am very much satisfied with. But before revealing that, I would like to get a little into what made me write this book.

The idea to even start this book stemmed from the fact that people today have are known to have very little attention span. The information you cram into 30 second videos are the only information that sits in our brains. When thinking about this, I felt like this should be applied to literature as well. Something that is short but does not compromise on the value the content provides. When thinking about a way to achieve this, I realised that every story has two sides. But every story also has a million interpretations. The ways we can play with these interpretations as writers is the most fascinating thing. The human brain's way to comprehend and understand things we read, but the fact that every brain does that differently, that is the very fact I decided to focus on.

As a teacher who handles small kids, I witness the way children these days, and in turn, the future generations will consume media. Bed time stories used to be a pivotal learning lessons when growing up. Those stories taught almost all morals that a lot of people carry with them today. But there is no one to tell kids stories like that today, or kids are not interested in listening to them. Reading would be of great help too. Reading imparts knowledge and perspective like no other activity can do. No other person can teach you things that you learn by reading and understanding things by yourself. The number of people who read today has drastically reduced. No one reads, even for the fun of reading. Either people do not have the time to sit and read a 300 page novel, or they cannot sit and read for that long. The only reason I see people, or rather, students reading today is for their English subject in school, and that too, just so that they get the marks they need to pass or make their parents happy.

As someone whose first language is not English, my immediate, almost reflexive, reaction when reading novels or anything in English is to compare it to my first language. In Tamil, we use a lot of proverbs and metaphor-like sentences in our day-to-day vocabulary and interactions. Seeing that this is missing in English interactions, wanting to incorporate that and use a lot of it in my work was also a huge reason for me to come up with this idea.

The genre that birthed from all these amalgamations of ideas is what I would like to call "METANAFIC." The word itself is an amalgamation of Metaphor, Narrative and Fiction. All my works in this book will be a melting pot of all these genres / writing styles. This book comprises of 25 works, which will be easy to read and has a meaning that can be taken from the text as is. But underneath every work, there will be small note to replace certain words with other words. Replacing those words will result in a new story with a new meaning and almost capturing a new emotion.

This was a very unconventional way of writing, but like I mentioned before, I feel like this captures all the ideas and thoughts flowing in my head and bring it to paper. More than just writing down what I feel like this preface, I wanted to put my creativity to use and bring in a new aspect that, I hope, people will enjoy reading. My goal for this book is to make people love reading again, not for marks or for work, but for the sake of reading.

As a literature student myself, I wish for this book to be something that changes the path in which we view literature. I wish this would encourage children and future generations to fall in love with reading like a lot of my classmates and I did. With that, I hope this book is something you enjoy spending your time reading.

Acknowledgements

I would like to express my heartfelt gratitude to my professor. Dr. Samuel Rufus for your constructive motivation and support. Your words of appreciation always motivated me a lot.

I extend my sincere thanks to prof. Dr. David Wesley for making me think different and always been a source of inspiration to me. I extend my sincere gratitude to all my Professors of the department of English.

I'm so blessed and thankful for my brother Jayaprakash for approving the contents I write and was always on point. I would like to thank Kavin nallarasu and Lekhaa M. S for their encouragement and thought provoking discussions.

Special thanks to Megha Sumesh my friend, who helped me a lot to make this book, I am so grateful for you. I am obliged to T Abraham who helped a lot to publish this book.

At last, I would like to extend my heartfelt thanks and sincere appreciation to my proof reader and editor, Nitish Kumar R K. Without you this book would've been nothing. Thank you so much.

Finally, I would always extend my appreciation to all my friends, my juniors, my wards and my family for guiding me patiently all through the process.

This new genre wouldn't have been possible without the collective efforts of these individuals. I'm always grateful for their presence. Thank you all personally.

Demo

A room without books is like a body without a soul.

-Marcus Tullius Cicero

(Replace Room with Man and books with Morals)

A Man without morals is like a body without a soul.

CHAPTER ONE

The Woe of a Social butterfly

A little butterfly discerns beauty in everything that she encounters while soaring gracefully above her wings. The young butterfly brings joy to those around her but harbours a profound sadness for the absent cocoon within her. Despite being aware that the cocoon is no more, the young butterfly struggles to come to terms with this reality. Eventhough the cocoon can never be retrieved, the young butterfly's yearning and hope seems to be never ending.

[Replace the Butterfly with a young girl and cocoon with her father]

CHAPTER TWO

Bicyclic nature

Upon getting new bicycle, I was so happy with that, I spent time with it everyday in delight, meanwhile my old bicycle felt abandoned before me. It is the old bicycle who stood beside me during terrifying events in the past and helped me. I could remember the day my new bicycle betrayed me in my need and my old bicycle without any hesitation stood ready to assist me arms wide.

[Replace New Bicycle with Money and Old Bicycle with Parents]

CHAPTER THREE

Illuminating your love

Once, in a room, there was a broken candle, a matchstick and several other objects, while the matchstick interacted amiably with the other objects, the broken candle remained isolated and anxious. This concern prompted the matchstick to initiate a conversation with the broken candle, as they grew closer, they eventually became good friends. Later, when the room was enveloped in darkness due to power outage, the other objects sought refuge by hiding themselves. In contrast, the matchstick and the broken candle lit up the room together, illuminating it entirely. The light not only faded the darkness of the room but also the sorrow of the broken candle.

[Replace the Broken Candle with Broken Heart, Matchstick with a Pure Soul and other objects with other people]

CHAPTER FOUR

Untold love tale

An enchanting love tale unfolds between the cactus and the full moon. The cactus starts flowering as a result of love upon witnessing the night, unfortunately their fleeting love lasts only a few hours until the hint of dawn, where they must part ways. With the blooms fading away the cactus eagerly awaits for their next night to reunite.

[Replace the Cactus with Motivative Thoughts and Full Moon with Night and Dawn with Sleep]

CHAPTER FIVE

Ones bastion

Upon a dark and haunting night, I inadvertently wandered down the wrong path, which took me deep into the woods eventually leading me to a dense thicket. On clearing the bushes, I stumbled to meet upon an impressive and grand castle with a majestic appearance. Despite my initial hesitations, I felt myself compelled to enter. Eventhough my fears initially lingered, the castle seemed to welcome me. As I journeyed through the various ups and downs like tunnels, this appeared to me as if the whole nature is contained inside this castle. I found myself reluctant to leave this castle, yearning for an eternal night and impatiently anticipating a sunrise after millennia.

[Replace Castle with Friend and Eternal Night with Eternal Bond]

CHAPTER SIX

The Fabric and Fabricator

The wet fabric after much cleansing was hung free and secluded tight by the clamp. The wet fabric struggles against the tight grip of the clamp, yearning for freedom. But once the wet fabric is released from the clamp, even the fabric becomes ugly and a burden to the owner and the society.

[Replace the Clamp with Parents and Wet Fabric with Teenager]

CHAPTER SEVEN

Not the regular cloud nine

I never witnessed such a pristine beauty of clouds ever before, until those hiccups arose in me. I used to pacify them always but one day suddenly everything around me seemed so beautiful after one such hiccups. I questioned myself it may be the clouds possess the same beauty and its me who never noticed them. After that incident, it transformed me, to a better version that I should thank those hiccups in transforming me for who I am now.

[Replace the Clouds with Life, Hiccups with those Tough Times]

CHAPTER EIGHT

Counting steorra

During a casual gathering on the terrace, a group of friends started conversing on stars and found themselves exhausted on seeing millions of stars. However they decided to count on the stars before them. Interestingly, every individual were drawn to different star finding it unique and captivating. Each of them found one peculiar star for their own and as a result they started to excel in their tasks. The life seems difficult for everyone until they figure out their own peculiar star, out of those millions of stars.

[Replace Millions of Stars with Opportunities and Peculiar Star with Skills]

CHAPTER NINE

Tele – Vision

Whenever we turn on to TV, we expect our favourite film/ favourite song to appear on our screen but that doesn't happen every time. But once that coincides with our thoughts, we turn ourselves from the outside world and peep into our favourite world.

[Replace TV with Sleep, screen with Dreams and Favourite Song/Film with Unsatisfied Moments/Progress]

CHAPTER TEN

Tailess lizard

A Tailess Lizard lost his tail as an aftermath of his mistake. Unknowingly roams here and there. The Mother Lizard notices this and waits peacefully with much hope for its child's regrowth on lost tail, and transformation in New life.

[Replace Tailess Lizard with a Student and Mother Lizard with a Responsible Teacher]

CHAPTER ELEVEN

Tot's mind; Thoughts in mind

Similar to how a child can't handle the prolonged curiosity of a surprise gift out of anticipation of what that could be, it would think on multiple unreal things. Finally with deep awakenment, it would go pitch to its parents and numb them until the child satisfies the longing.

[Replace the Curiosity of a Surprise Gift to Happiness and Parents to our Past Memories, Child to Human Mind]

CHAPTER TWELVE

Valuable stuffs

Two friends engaged in a dispute over the value of a coal versus a diamond. To settle their disagreement, they sought the counsel of a prophet and the prophecy revealed that both substances were essentially same. Their value is determined by the individual possessing them and from that moment the coal was also considered equivalent to the diamond. In the end not only there was a change mindset of the friends but they also realised the value of their bonds.

[Replace the Coal with Calendar and Diamond with Diary]

CHAPTER THIRTEEN

Seasonal Phase

It was time for the winter and everyone chased the summer away. They accused summer for drying the river, but they didn't know that the summer dried the river just for the winter to fill in abundantly.

[Replace Summer with Scream, River with Heart and Winter with Happy Tears]

CHAPTER FOURTEEN

Stage of life

Every single property that we come across on stage has its own significance. It can be a small property, but even this can create a huge impact on stage. That small property can be the reason for the rise or fall of a character.

[Replace Property with Incident and Stage with Life]

CHAPTER FIFTEEN

Just the two

The Sand clock seems majestic, until one keenly observes the sand discerning from the top tier and reaches the bottom tier, and again when you flip, reaching the initial positions descends again. I'm sure it will change something in you.

[Replace Sandclock with Universe, Top Tier with Heaven, Bottom Tier with Earth, Sand with life]

CHAPTER SIXTEEN

When second speaks

In the world where Second chances are valued, while second positions are overlooked people tend to appreciate second chances but neglect acknowledging those who've worked hard to achieve the victory. Personally, I believe that both Second chances and Second positions are equally important, yet often go unnoticed by many.

[Replace Second Chances with Victory and Second Positions with efforts]

CHAPTER SEVENTEEN

The wealth I posses

When people left me thinking of just sand, they went without knowing the indepth gold I posses, but when that one person who looked deep in me, besides the outer filth, he noticed the gold within the sand. And then, besides the gold, he started to love the sand more than the gold.

[Replace the sand with imperfections and gold with Golden character]

CHAPTER EIGHTEEN

Budding actor

The bug came across a garden and found a flower. He approached the flower and began to extract honey. After he succeeded the task, the bug lingered, remaining in the flower for some time. He stayed in the flower for a while, that shows the worth of the flower; this is common in the world of nature.

[Replace bug with Actor, Garden with stage, flower with character, extract honey with perform, Nature with art]

CHAPTER NINETEEN

Gushing but worth it

Water can be the best example of adaptability.Water can adapt according to the container.People often consider water for granted, but the same people forget that water can be the best elixir. Just ponder before taking for granted.

[Replace water with extroverts and elixir with listeners and container with environment]

CHAPTER TWENTY

Unnoticed gems

Some saplings aspire to grow and reach great heights by attaining their fruits; some succeed, while the others cease and deviate in their halfway for other tasks. Those deviated saplings suppress their pain, prepare for their new tasks, and try to excel in them. However, their pain often goes unnoticed and gets buried inside them in silence.

[Replace saplings with individuals fruits with goals and tasks with works]

CHAPTER TWENTY-ONE

From my abyss

Once, I heard about Gaia and Uranus and it seemed to me that they loved each other with intense passion. Both loved profoundly to the extent where God himself thought to test their passion and distanced each other to both extremes. Since Gaia cannot extend to the Uranus and the Uranus too cannot reach Gaia. But the irony is that, they never changed because of their very nature. Their true love and passion exists till now and is still spoken by many.

[Replace Gaia with rose sapling and Uranus with abyss]

CHAPTER TWENTY-TWO

Aren't you exhausted?

Hey, waves aren't you tired? Won't you ever feel worn out? You come to shore constantly without any break, sometimes with large waves, sometimes with small ones but you never stop reaching me and pour out your love on me endlessly. Aren't you even a bit exhausted? Whenever I ask you this question, you answer me with a smile, filled with zillion love. I think this is why every people love you and hold you close to their heart among others.

[Replace waves with mom, shore with me, large waves with love, small ones with anger]

CHAPTER TWENTY-THREE

An Artisan's Silence

As an artist, I felt like the best artist in this artistic world. I tried to use every color to please this art and prove myself. One moment, all of a sudden, all those colors in my palette seemed so different to me. 'It's going to mess up,' my intuition said. My hands shivered, my brush out of control, mixed and messed up every color I had. All those colors wanted to prove their supremacy, but everything paved the way for one solution; suddenly, everything seemed calm and composed in me. And that is "Black". It wasn't my fault, and no one is going to believe it, but this black is ready to accompany me for my future artworks.

[Replace artist with Individual, colours with people,palette with surrounding, brush with mind, Black with Silence]

CHAPTER TWENTY-FOUR

The Serendipity it holds

Have you ever thought of your favourite food? They can always be in your mind; they never bore you and is strong enough to change your mind within seconds. They're more special when you think about them and the feel it gives you when you think about them can't be described with puny words. Its more than what you actually feel when you taste that food. The feeling of not being able to express how it feels says the love the favourite food holds. Likewise, some of the unexpressed stuffs in our life hold more feelings and connection.

[Replace favourite food with favourite person, taste with express, food with bond]

CHAPTER TWENTY-FIVE

Gentle Gaintess

She was born somewhere, came to me on one grand day and we hardly had much conversations. Why is this elephant so loyal to me?..She spares her life for me, ready to die for me and my victory. The elephant is so soft in nature when she came to me, she never raised her voice to me, but when it comes to my safety, she turns wild. For me she is just animal too young in age but her nature is too senior and delicate from mine. Is this love inbuilt in her nature or just a gratitude?..Staring at the elephant, the chieftain whispered these in his mind.

[Replace elephant with girl, an Animal with my wife, chieftain with Husband]

After Replacement

CHAPTER TWENTY-SIX

Replaced Versions

1. The Woe of a Social Butterfly

A little young girl discerns beauty in everything that she encounters while soaring gracefully above her wings. The little girl brings joy to those around her but harbours a profound sadness for the absent father within her. Despite being aware that the father is no more, the young girl struggles to come to terms with this reality. Eventhough the father can never be retrieved, the young girl's yearning and hope seems to be never ending.

2. Bicyclic Nature

Upon getting money, I was so happy with that, I spent time with it everyday in delight, meanwhile I my parents felt abandoned before me. It is the parents who stood beside me during terrifying events in the past and helped me. I could remember the day my money betrayed me in my need and my parents without any hesitation stood ready to assist me arms wide.

3. Illuminating your love

Once, in a room, there was a broken heart, a pure soul and several other people, while the pure soul interacted amiably with the other people, the broken heart remained isolated and anxious. This concern prompted the pure soul to initiate a conversation with the broken heart. As they grew closer, they eventually became good friends. Later, when the room was enveloped in darkness due to power outage, the other people sought refuge by hiding themselves. In contrast, the pure soul and the broken heart lit up the room together, illuminating it entirely. The light not only faded the darkness of the room but also the sorrow of the broken candle.

4. Untold love tale

An enchanting love tale unfolds between the motivative thoughts and the night. The motivative thoughts starts flowering as a result of love upon witnessing the night, unfortunately their fleeting love lasts only a few hours until the hint of sleep, where they must part ways. With the blooms fading away the motivative thoughts eagerly awaits for their next night to reunite.

5. Once bastion

Upon a dark and haunting night, I inadvertently wandered down the wrong path, which took me deep into the woods eventually leading me to a dense thicket. On clearing the bushes, I stumbled to meet upon an impressive and grand friend with a majestic appearance. Despite my initial hesitations, I felt myself compelled to enter. Eventhough my fears initially lingered, the friend seemed to welcome me. As I journeyed through the various ups and downs like tunnels, this appeared to me as if the whole nature is contained inside this friend. I found myself reluctant to leave this friend, yearning for an eternal bond and impatiently anticipating a sunrise after millennia.

6. The Fabric and Fabricator

The teenager after much cleansing was hung free and secluded tight by the parents. The teenager struggles against the tight grip of the parents, yearning for freedom. But once the teenager is released from the parents, even the teenager becomes ugly and a burden to the owner and the society.

7. Not the regular cloud nine

I never witnessed such a pristine beauty of life ever before, until those tough times arose in me. I used to pacify them always but one day suddenly everything around me seemed so beautiful after one such tough times. I questioned myself it may be the life possess the same beauty and its me who never noticed them. After that incident, it transformed me, to a better version that I should thank those tough times in transforming me for who I am now.

8. Counting steorra

During a casual gathering on the terrace, a group of friends started conversing on skills and found themselves exhausted on seeing more opportunities. However they decided to count on the opportunities before them. Interestingly, every individual were drawn to different skills finding it unique and captivating. Each of them found one skills for their own and as a result they started to excel in their tasks. The life seems difficult for everyone until they figure out their own skills, out of those millions of opportunities.

9. Tele - Vision

Whenever we turn on to Sleep, we expect our Unsatisfied Moments/Progress to appear on our Dreams but that doesn't happen every time. But once that coincides with our thoughts, we turn ourselves from the outside world and peep into our favourite world.

10. Tailess Lizard

A student lost his tail as an aftermath of his mistake. Unknowingly roams here and there. The responsible teacher notices this and waits peacefully with much hope for its child's regrowth on lost tail, and transformation in New life.

11. Tot's mind; Thoughts in mind

Similar to how a human mind can't handle the prolonged happiness out of anticipation of what that could be, it would think on multiple unreal things. Finally with deep awakenment, it would go pitch to its past memories and numb them until the human mind satisfies the longing.

12. Valuable stuffs

Two friends engaged in a dispute over the value of a Calendar versus a Diary. To settle their disagreement, they sought the counsel of a prophet and the prophecy revealed that both substances were essentially same. Their value is determined by the individual possessing them and from that moment Calendar was also considered equivalent to the Diary. In the end not only there was a change in the mindset of the friends but they also realised the value of their bonds.

13. Seasonal phase

It was time for the happy tears and everyone chased the scream away. They accused scream for drying the heart, but they didn't know that the scream dried the heart just for the happy tears to fill in abundantly.

14. Stage of life

Every single incident that we come across on life has its own significance. It can be a small incident, but even this can create a huge impact on life. That small incident can be the reason for the rise or fall of a character.

15. Just the two

The Universe seems majestic, until one keenly observes the life discerning from the heaven and reaches the earth, and again when you flip, reaching the initial positions descends again. I'm sure it will change something in you.

16. When second speaks

In the world where victory are valued, while efforts are overlooked people tend to appreciate victory but neglect acknowledging those who've worked hard to achieve the victory. Personally, I believe that both victory and efforts are equally important, yet often go unnoticed by many.

17. The wealth I posses

When people left me thinking of just imperfections, they went without knowing the indepth golden character I posses, but when that one person who looked deep in me, besides the outer filth, he noticed the golden character within the imperfections. And then, besides the golden character, he started to love the imperfections more than the golden character.

18. Budding actor

The actor came across a stage and found a character. He approached the character and began to perform. After he succeeded the task, the actor lingered, remaining in the character for some time. He stayed in the character for a while, that shows the worth of the character; this is common in the world of art.

19. Gushing but worth it

Extroverts can be the best example of adaptability. Extroverts can adapt according to the environment. People often consider extroverts for granted, but the same people forget that extroverts can be the best listeners. Just ponder before taking for granted.

20. Unnoticed gems

Some individuals aspire to grow and reach great heights by attaining their goals; some succeed, while the others cease and deviate in their halfway for other works. Those deviated individual suppress their pain, prepare for their new works, and try to excel in them. However, their pain often goes unnoticed and gets buried inside them in silence.

21. From my Abyss

Once, I heard about rose sapling and abyss and it seemed to me that they loved each other with intense passion. Both loved profoundly to the extent where God himself thought to test their passion and distanced each other to both extremes. Since rose sapling cannot extend to the abyss and the abyss too cannot reach rose sapling. But the irony is that, they never changed because of their very nature. Their true love and passion exists till now and is still spoken by many.

22. Aren't you exhausted?

Hey, mom aren't you tired? Won't you ever feel worn out? You come to me constantly without any break, sometimes with love, sometimes with anger but you never stop reaching me and pour out your love on me endlessly. Aren't you even a bit exhausted? Whenever I ask you this question, you answer me with a smile, filled with zillion love. I think this is why every people love you and hold you close to their heart among others.

23. An Artisan's Silence

As an individual, I felt like the best individual in this artistic world. I tried to use every people to please this art and prove myself. One moment, all of a sudden, all those people in my surrounding seemed so different to me. 'It's going to mess up,' my intuition said. My hands shivered, my mind out of control, mixed and messed up every people I had. All those people wanted to prove their supremacy, but everything paved the way for one solution; suddenly, everything seemed calm and composed in me. And that is "Silence". It wasn't my fault, and no one is going to believe it, but this silence is ready to accompany me for my future artworks.

24. The Serendipity it holds

Have you ever thought of your favourite person? They can always be in your mind; they never bore you and is strong enough to change your mind within seconds. They're more special when you think about them and the feel it gives you when you think about them cannot be described with puny words. Its more than what you actually feel when you express that bond. The feeling of not being able to express how it feels says the love the favourite person holds. Likewise, some of the unexpressed stuffs in our life hold more feelings and connection

25. Gentle Gaintess

She was born somewhere, came to me on one grand day and we hardly had much conversations. Why is this girl so loyal to me?. She spares her life for me, ready to die for me and my victory. The girl is so soft in nature when she came to me, she never raised her voice to me, but when it comes to my safety, she turns wild. For me she is just my wife too young in age but her nature is too senior and delicate from mine. Is this love in built in her nature or just a gratitude?..Staring at the girl, the husband whispered these in his mind.

Author's Bio

As students of literature, we see a lot of people who have a way with words. But it is not often that we witness these writers actually put their works out for the world to read while we are still studying.Veena is one of the few who made that possible. She is very enthusiastic about literature in itself, which reflects in her academic excellence. But apart from that, she is very passionate about the art of reading in itself. Her friends recall her finishing a book within thethree hours she can spare for herself in a day. At this young age, she has mastered the balance between studies and life and she has made sure to incorporate her passion for writing into this balance. This book stands testament to her love for writing and her curiosity to explore various ideas. She has made a strong mark for herself, her first work exploring a whole new genre. She is one of the most promising writers with the mind to make her ideas a reality. It is with this mentality that she will reach more success in life.

She is currently studying English literature at Madras Christian College and it is her love for literature that gave birth to this idea. I am genuinely in awe of her accomplishments and wish her only the best from here on.

P.S: Her book is really good! I hope you all enjoy it as much as I did.

www.ingramcontent.com/pod-product-compliance
Lightning Source LLC
LaVergne TN
LVHW090135160826
845673LV00017B/2472